Barbie ™

Look, Listen, and Learn

Preschool Workbook

Modern Publishing
A Division of Unisystems, Inc.
New York, New York 10022
Series UPC #49910
Printed in the U.S.A.

D1205257

Modern Publishing
A Division of Unisystems, Inc.
New York, New York 10022

Dear Parents:

Help your child get a head start with the **Barbie™ Preschool Workbooks**!

The activities in this friendly, entertaining workbook were created by educational experts to introduce your child to the concepts and essential skills of early learning. You will find that working along with Barbie and her friends is a wonderful way to encourage your child's enthusiasm for learning. These books can also help your child build self-esteem and social skills while reinforcing the fundamentals of reading, writing, mathematics, and reasoning.

These suggestions can help make your time together more rewarding:
♡ Work in a quiet place.
♡ Discuss each page before you start.
♡ Give your child time to think about the activity.
♡ If your child loses interest in a page, stop or go on to another.
♡ Give your child a lot of praise—and be specific.
♡ Provide a selection of writing instruments (pencils, markers, or crayons).
♡ Help your child relate the activities to everyday life.
♡ Enjoy the time together!

This title, *LOOK, LISTEN, AND LEARN*, teaches the following essential skills:
♡ developing writing readiness and fine motor skills
♡ reading upper- and lowercase letters in alphabetical order
♡ determining initial consonant sounds and rhyming sounds
♡ recognizing shapes, colors, and the words that describe them
♡ counting sets and writing numbers from 1 to 10
♡ comparing size (big/small) and quantity (more/less)
♡ noticing details, similarities, and differences

Essential Skills

The activities presented in *Look, Listen, and Learn* were carefully planned to meet the needs of preschool children. Each chapter offers children the opportunity to practice basic skills that can serve as a foundation for future learning.

🤍 Look and Match

Barbie encourages children to **stretch their thinking skills; use visual perception; identify identical objects; find parts of a whole object;** and **observe differences in position.**

🤍 Thinking and Comparing

Barbie asks children to **use logical reasoning; classify objects into categories; understand the concept of quantity; think creatively;** and **make size comparisons.**

🤍 Writing the Alphabet

Barbie teaches children to **match letters and sounds; develop fine motor skills; trace uppercase letters; write from left to right;** and **understand letter order.**

🤍 Colors and Shapes

Barbie and her friends help children to **identify colors; distinguish geometric shapes; recognize written color and shape names;** and **notice shapes and colors in everyday life.**

🤍 Numbers

Barbie helps children to **count from 1 to 10; understand number order; create and match sets; recognize written numerals from 1 to 10;** and **trace and write numerals.**

🤍 Letters and Sounds

Barbie encourages children to **recognize alphabetical order; match written letters to sounds; hear differences between letters; distinguish uppercase and lowercase; identify beginning consonants;** and **write letters.**

🤍 Words and More Words

Barbie teaches children to **match pictures to simple words; see correspondences between spoken and written words; practice left-to-right reading; understand pairs of related words;** and **identify opposites.**

Table of Contents

Look and Match

With help from Barbie and her friends, children can look, listen, and learn every day. This chapter encourages them to stretch their thinking skills with a variety of activities, including:

- using visual perception skills
- finding similarities between objects
- matching objects that are identical
- recognizing differences
- finding parts of a whole object
- observing differences in position.

Recognizing Differences

Matching

Noticing Details

LOOK AND MATCH

Barbie and Teresa are good friends.
They are going shopping together to buy matching outfits.
Look at the clothes on this page.
Draw lines to show which clothes are exactly the **same**.

Skills: Visual discrimination; Finding similarities; Friendship

Kelly is collecting shells on the beach.
Look at each group of shells she found.
Cross out the one that is **different** in each group.

Skills: Visual discrimination; Finding differences; Nature; Curiosity

Barbie takes good care of the flowers in her garden.
Look at the flower in each box below.
Then look at the detail in each small box.
Find that detail in the large picture and circle it.

Skills: Visual discrimination; Finding parts of a whole; Noticing details; Nature; Caring

Barbie and her friends like to share purses that come in many shapes.
Look at each row of shapes.
Circle the shape that is in a different position from the others.

Skills: Visual discrimination; Recognizing differences; Understanding directionality; Friendship; Sharing

LOOK AND MATCH

Barbie is a beautiful ballerina!
She needs strong muscles for dancing.
Look at all her costumes.
Draw lines to match each picture with the correct shadow.

Skills: Visual discrimination; Finding differences; Noticing details; Fitness

LOOK AND MATCH

Barbie is Ken's track coach.
She is helping him get ready to run in a race.
Look at what she brought along.
Circle one object in each box that is **different** from the others.

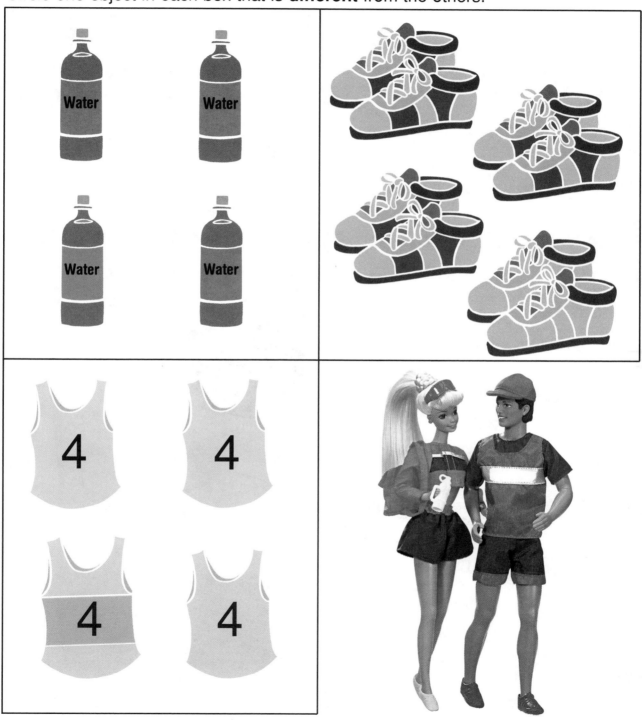

Skills: Visual discrimination; Finding differences; Noticing details; Cooperation; Fitness

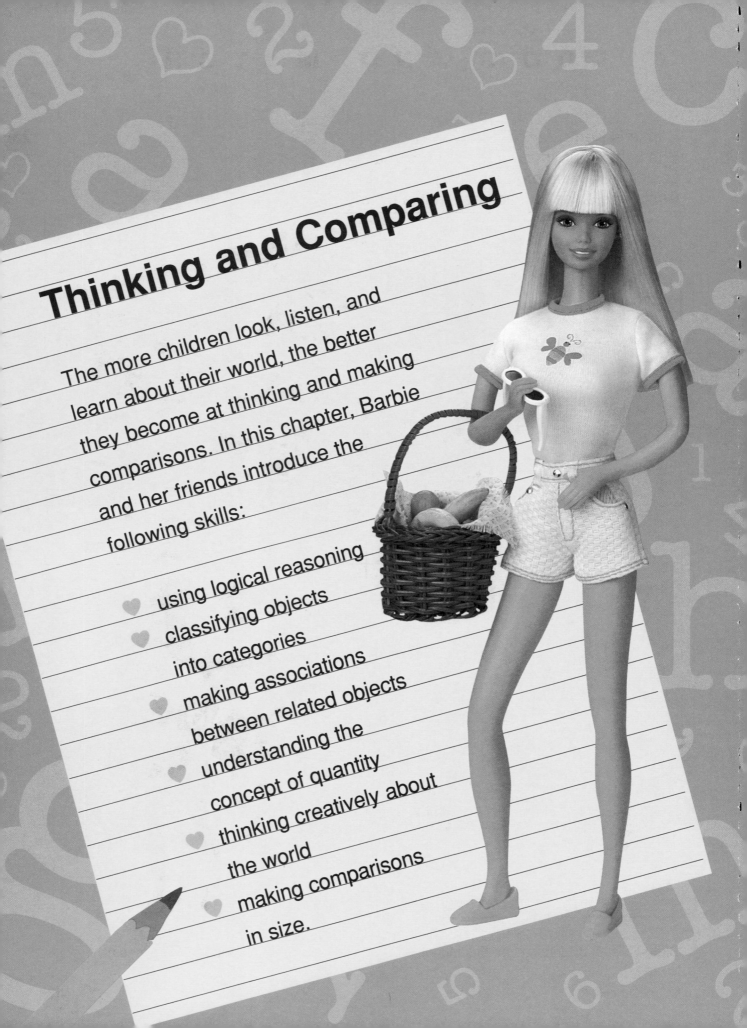

Thinking and Comparing

The more children look, listen, and learn about their world, the better they become at thinking and making comparisons. In this chapter, Barbie and her friends introduce the following skills:

- using logical reasoning
- classifying objects into categories
- making associations between related objects
- understanding the concept of quantity
- thinking creatively about the world
- making comparisons in size.

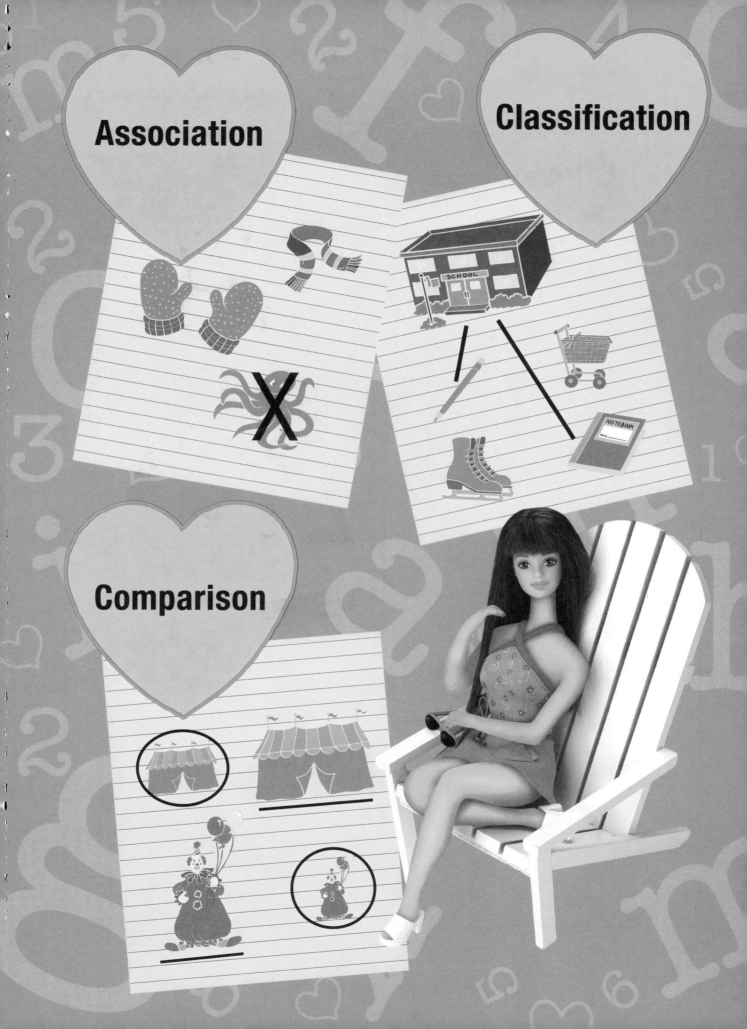

Association

Classification

Comparison

Ken is helping his neighbor to clean out the garage.
Look at each group of objects he found.
Circle the two pictures that go together.

Skills: Association; Logical reasoning; Helping; Community

THINKING AND COMPARING

Stacie is packing her bookbag for school.
She doesn't want to forget anything important!
Circle the pictures of things she should take to school.
Draw an **X** over the things she should leave at home.

Skills: Association; Classification; Logical reasoning; Responsibility

Barbie, Ken, and Stacie are having lunch at their campsite.
Stacie is roasting marshmallows for everyone.
Circle all the other things they might eat on a camping trip.

Skills: Classification; Logical reasoning; Friendship; Sharing; Nature

© 1999 Mattel, Inc.

Kelly is smaller than Barbie.
Kelly wants to know which pets are smaller.
Look at each pair of animals.
Circle the one that is **smaller**.
Draw a line under the one that is **larger**.

Skills: Making comparisons; Logical reasoning; Curiosity; Family

Teresa works in a hair salon. She counts the supplies every day.
Look at each group of pictures.
Draw a line under the group in each box that shows **more**.
Circle the group that shows **less**.

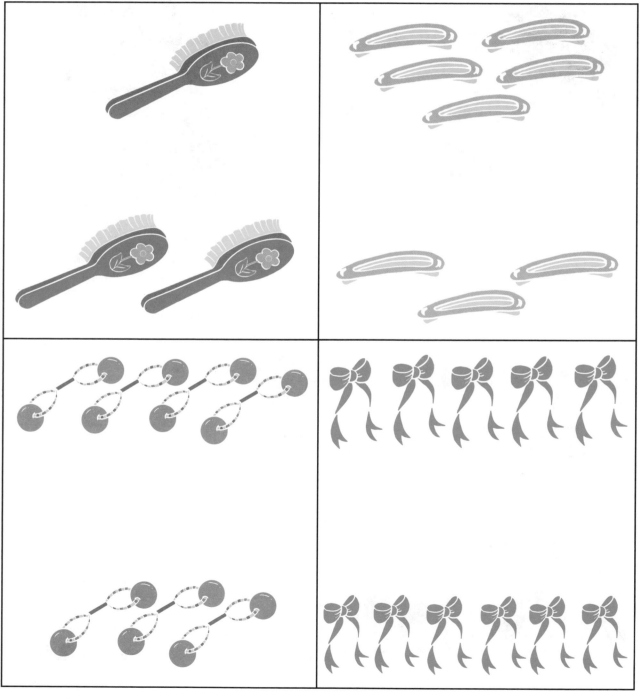

Skills: Making comparisons; Logical reasoning; Responsibility

It's moving day! Ken is helping Barbie by loading up the car.
Look at each picture.
Circle the pictures of things that could fit in the car.

Skills: Classification; Logical reasoning; Inference; Friendship; Helping

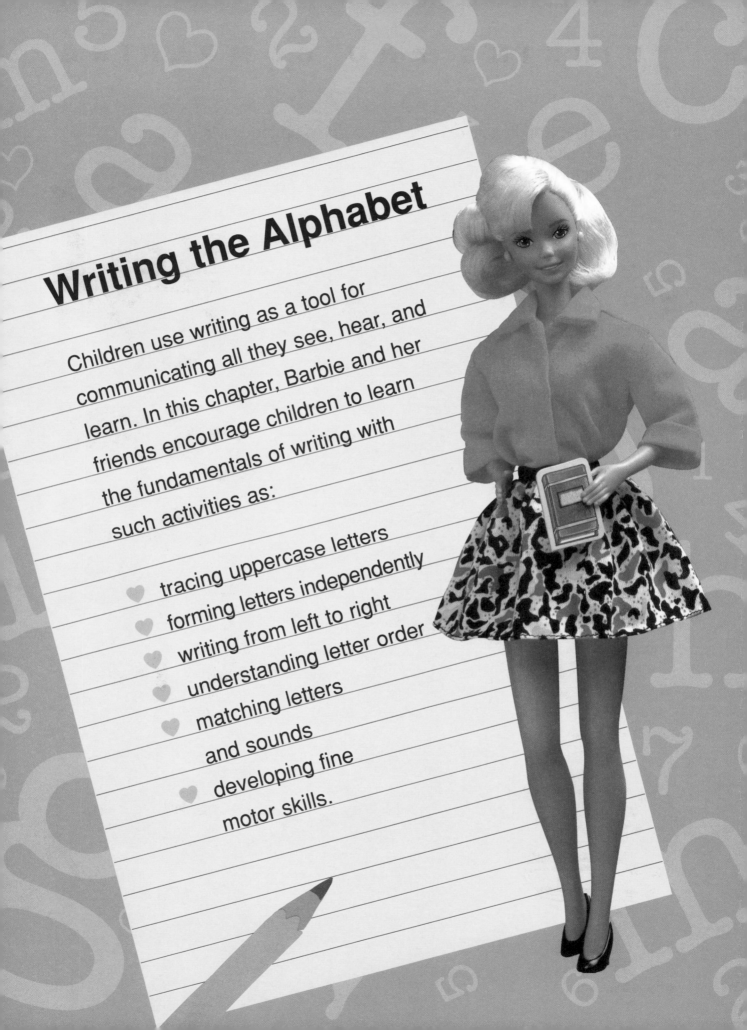

Writing the Alphabet

Children use writing as a tool for communicating all they see, hear, and learn. In this chapter, Barbie and her friends encourage children to learn the fundamentals of writing with such activities as:

- tracing uppercase letters
- forming letters independently
- writing from left to right
- understanding letter order
- matching letters and sounds
- developing fine motor skills.

Matching Sounds
K
T
Writing Uppercase Letters
P
D
Letter Sounds
B
L
S

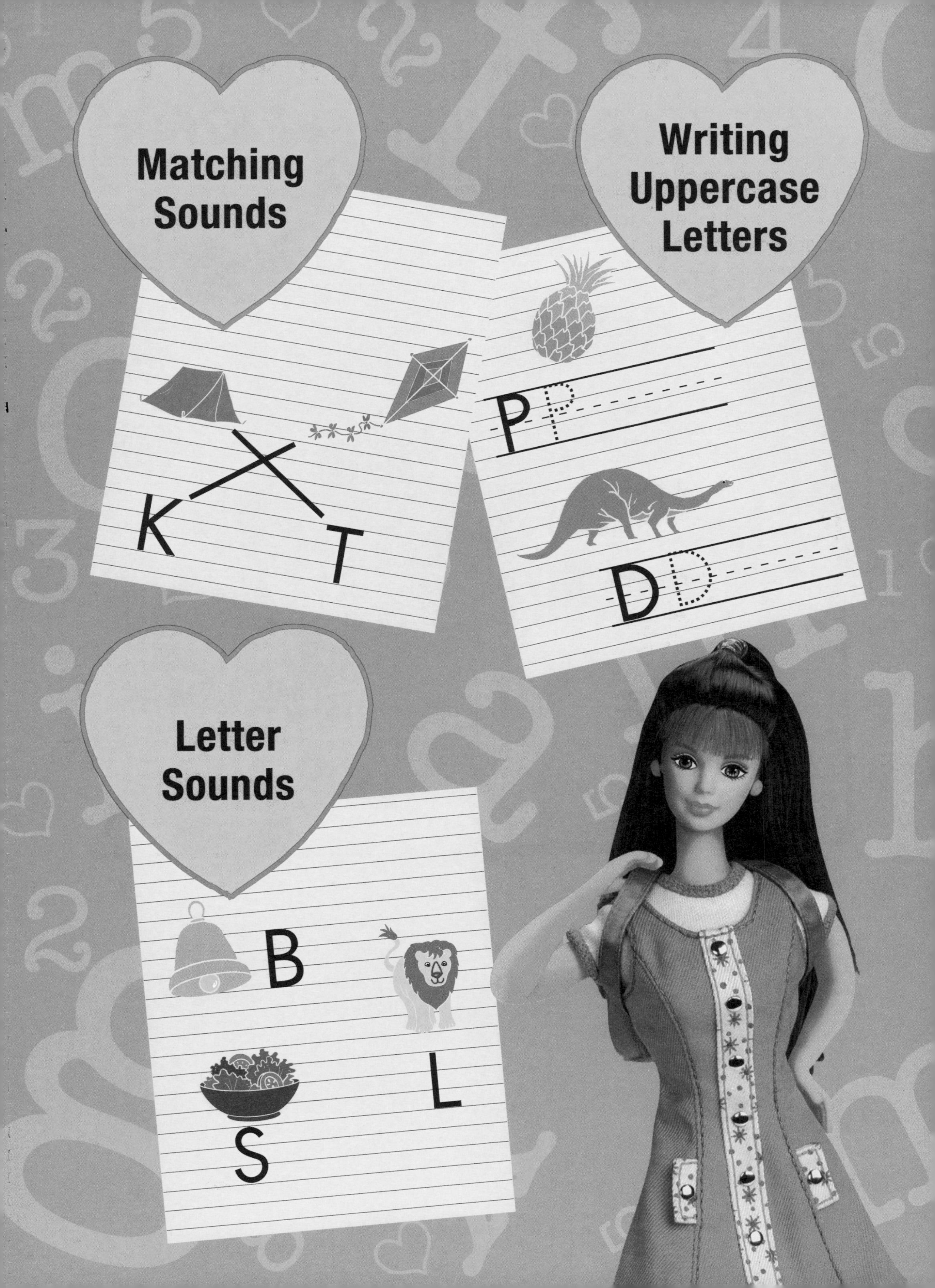

Kelly is looking at an alphabet book.
She points to an **A**nt, a **B**ear, a **C**amel, and a **D**og.
Help her learn the letters by naming each animal.
What sound does each name begin with?
Then trace and write each letter.

Skills: Recognizing letters; Fine motor skills; Eye-hand coordination; Curiosity

Barbie is shopping at Midge's Grocery Store.
Midge tells Barbie where she can find **E**ggs, **F**ish, **G**rapes, and **H**oney.
Can you say each letter name and write each letter?

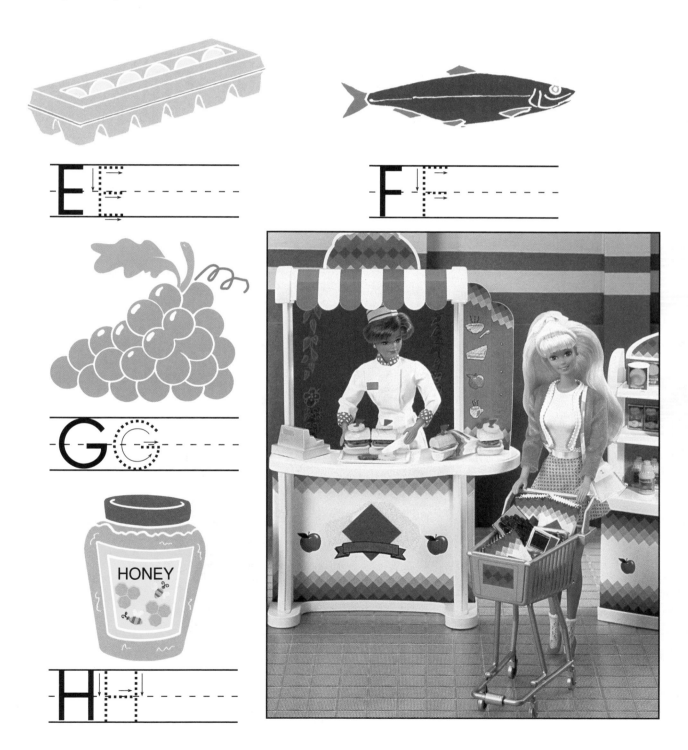

Skills: Recognizing letters; Fine motor skills; Eye-hand coordination; Helping

Barbie is always doing something fun!
She likes to **I**ce skate, **J**uggle, fly **K**ites, and **L**eap.
Can you say each letter name and write each letter?

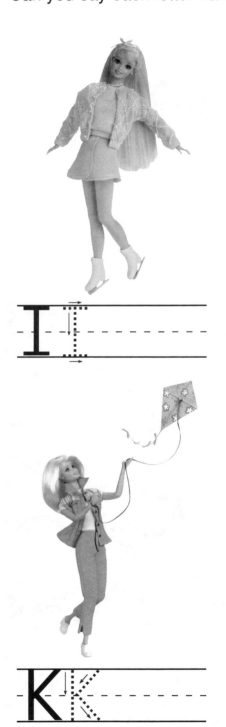

I

J

K

L

Skills: Recognizing letters; Fine motor skills; Eye-hand coordination; Fitness

Ken sold all of his string beans at the farmer's market!
He bought food as well.
He chose **M**ushrooms, **N**uts, **O**nions, and **P**ears.
Can you say each letter name and write each letter?

M M M

N N N

O O

P P

Skills: Recognizing letters; Fine motor skills; Eye-hand coordination; Responsibility

Barbie is the decorator for a new apartment.
She picked out a new **Q**uilt, the **R**ug, the **S**ign, and the **T**able.
Can you say each letter name and write each letter?

Q

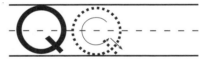

S

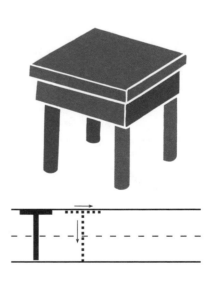

T

Skills: Recognizing letters; Fine motor skills; Eye-hand coordination; Creativity

Barbie cannot forget her **U**mbrella, **V**an, and **W**atch!
She drives to school to show the children how to
play the **X**ylophone.
Can you say each letter name and write each letter?

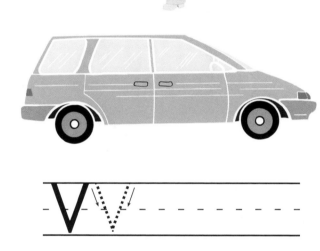

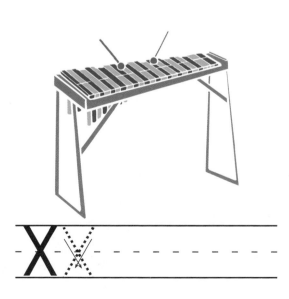

Skills: Recognizing letters; Fine motor skills; Eye-hand coordination; Responsibility

Barbie made this cool sweater for Christie.
She knitted it with **Y**arn. It has a **Z**ig-zag stripe.
Can you say each letter name and write each letter?

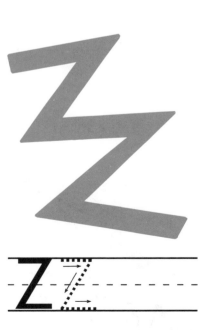

Skills: Recognizing letters; Fine motor skills; Eye-hand coordination; Friendship; Generosity; Creativity

Kelly's favorite lunch is Barbie's homemade alphabet soup.
Look in the bowl. Trace the letters Kelly sees.

Skills: Tracing letters; Fine motor skills; Family

Colors and Shapes

When they look, listen, and learn, children find a world filled with wonderful shapes and colors. In this chapter, Barbie and her friends encourage children to practice many important skills:

- identifying primary and secondary colors
- distinguishing simple geometric shapes
- differentiating similar shapes
- recognizing the names of colors and shapes
- using fine motor skills to color in shapes
- noticing shapes and colors in everyday life.

Matching Shapes

Colors

Shape and Color Words

Blue

Circle

COLORS AND SHAPES

Barbie is playing basketball in the pool. The ball is a red **circle**.
Look at the shapes below. Color all the circles **red.**

Skills: Recognizing colors and shapes; Noticing shapes in objects; Visual discrimination; Fitness

Barbie is giving Ken a tour of the art museum.
They see a painting that is a blue **square.**
Look at the shapes below. Color all the squares **blue.**

Skills: Recognizing colors and shapes; Noticing shapes in objects; Visual discrimination; Curiosity; Friendship

What a sunny day!
Barbie is on the deck.
The pennants behind her are **triangles.**
Look at the shapes below.
Color all the triangles **yellow.**

Skills: Recognizing colors and shapes; Noticing shapes in objects; Visual discrimination

Librarian Barbie loves to read books.
This book is a purple **rectangle**.
Look at the shapes below. Color all the rectangles **purple**.

Skills: Recognizing colors and shapes; Noticing shapes in objects; Visual discrimination

Officer Ken is on patrol near the fence in the park.
The green fence has sections that are **diamond**-shaped.
Look at the shapes below. Color all the diamonds **green**.

Skills: Recognizing colors and shapes; Noticing shapes in objects; Visual discrimination;
Helping; Community

Todd fell down and broke his leg.
Maybe a lollipop will cheer him up!
This orange lollipop is **oval**.
Look at all the shapes below.
Color all the ovals **orange**.

Skills: Recognizing colors and shapes; Noticing shapes in objects; Visual discrimination; Friendship; Sensitivity

© 1999 Mattel, Inc.

Numbers

Numbers are one of the world's most important tools. Children will look, listen, and learn as Barbie and her friends guide them through this chapter of fundamental early math skills, such as:

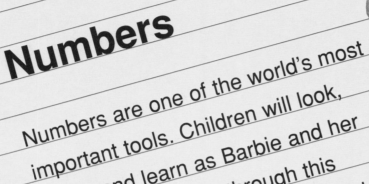

- counting from 1 to 10
- understanding number order
- creating and matching sets
- identifying quantities from 1 to 10
- recognizing written numerals from 1 to 10
- tracing and writing numerals.

Writing Numerals

Counting

1

2

④ 5 6

Creating Sets

7

Barbie is visiting the animals on the farm.
Count the number of each animal. Then name the numbers below.
Trace and write each number.

Skills: Writing the numerals 1-5; Counting amounts to 5; Fine motor skill development; Nature

NUMBERS

Stacie and her friend are organizing their school supplies.
Count the number of objects.
Then name the numbers below.
Trace and write each number.

Skills: Writing the numerals 6-10; Counting amounts to 10; Fine motor skill development; Responsibility; Friendship

Barbie listens to the weather report on the radio.
What will the weather be?
Look at the weather pictures below.
Circle the number that tells how many of each you see.

Skills: Recognizing sets and the corresponding numeral; Counting amounts to 10

Barbie is buying a birthday gift for Stacie.
There are so many toys to choose from.
Count the toys on each shelf.
Write how many in the space at the end of the row.

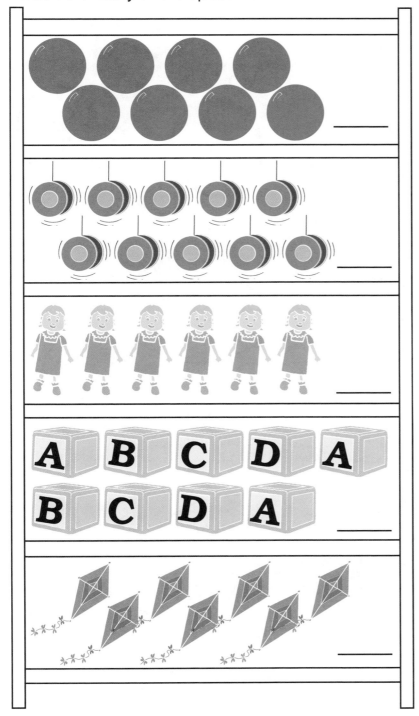

Skills: Recognizing sets and the corresponding numeral; Counting amounts to 10; Writing numerals; Family; Generosity

Barbie follows safety rules when she rides her bike. She watches out for people walking or driving cars. She always wears her helmet. She obeys traffic signs. Help her follow the correct path by tracing the numbers in order from **1** to **10**.

START

STOP

FINISH

Skills: Writing the numerals 1-10; Recognizing number order; Fine motor skill development; Counting; Fitness; Safety

NUMBERS

Christie is painting a picture for Barbie's house.
The numbers **1** to **10** are hidden in her studio.
Find and circle these numbers.

Skills: Counting; Recognizing numerals; Creativity; Friendship

Letters and Sounds

As they look, listen, and learn, children begin to relate written letters to the sounds they say and hear. In this chapter, Barbie and her friends help children with the following skills:

♥ recognizing alphabetical order

♥ matching written letters to letter sounds

♥ hearing differences between letter sounds

♥ distinguishing uppercase and lowercase letters

♥ identifying beginning consonant sounds

♥ writing letters to match sounds.

Upper and Lowercase Letters

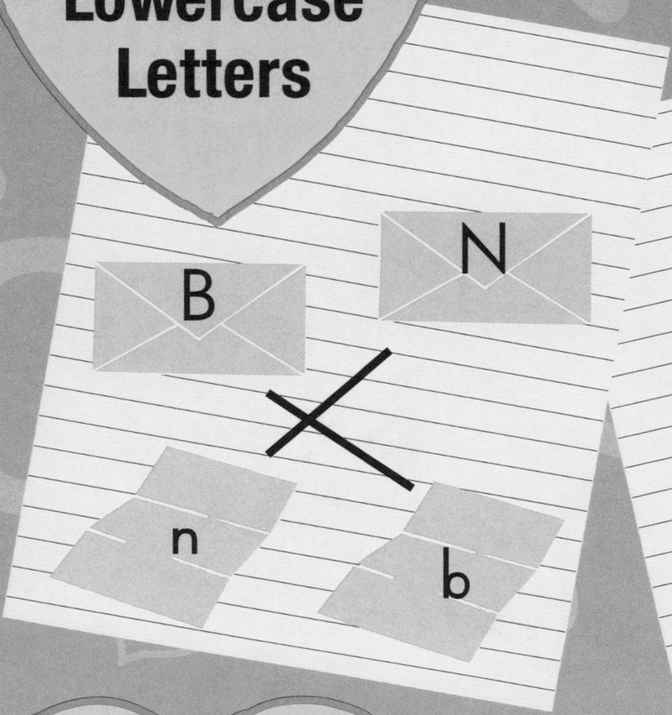

B

N

n

b

Letter Order

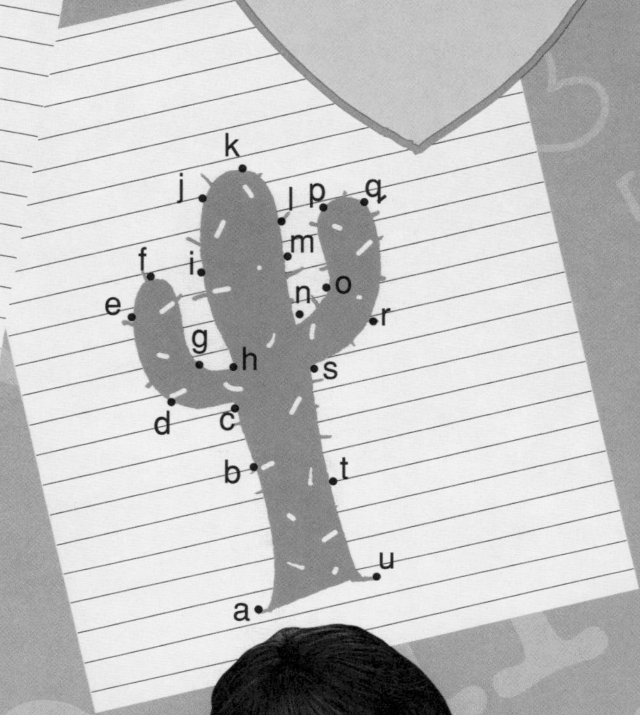

k
j
f   i   l   p   q
e   m
g   n   o
h   r
d   c   s
b   t

a   u

Letter Sounds

A

R

G

Barbie is on her way to meet Ken.
Follow the dots from **A** to **Z** to find out
what Barbie's new car looks like.

Skills: Ordering letters A-Z; Recognizing uppercase letters; Friendship

© 1999 Mattel, Inc.

Barbie and Kira are helping to clean up the park.
They see things that begin with the **S** sound, the **T** sound, and the **B** sound.
Look at the picture below. Circle the things whose names begin with **S**.
Draw a line under the things whose names begin with **B**.
Draw a box around the things whose names begin with **T**.

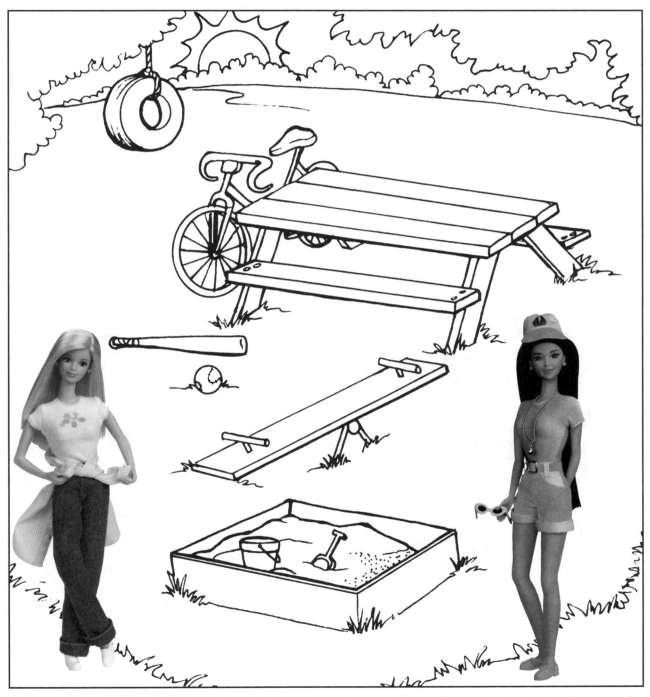

Skills: Auditory discrimination; Association of sounds and letters; Recognizing beginning sounds; Community; Helping

Barbie and Ken are camping.
They see things that begin with the **C** sound, the **R** sound, and the **W** sound.
Look at the picture below.
Circle the things whose names begin with **C**.
Draw a line under the things whose names begin with **W**.
Put a dot next to the things whose names begin with **R**.

Skills: Auditory discrimination; Association of sounds and letters; Recognizing beginning
sounds; Nature; Friendship

Kelly is drawing things that begin with the **K** sound,
the **H** sound, and the **M** sound.
Look at the pictures of things that she drew.
Write the sound you hear at the beginning of each pictured word.

Skills: Auditory discrimination; Association of sounds and letters; Recognizing beginning sounds;
Writing letters

Barbie is exploring a trail.
She makes sure the nature trail is safe.
Look at the pictures of things Barbie saw on the trail.
They begin with the **D** sound, the **N** sound, and the **L** sound.
Write the sound you hear at the beginning of each pictured word.

Skills: Auditory discrimination; Association of sounds and letters; Writing letters; Recognizing beginning sounds; Nature; Conservation; Safety

Skipper is in the school yard. She notices things that begin with the **J** sound, the **V** sound, and the **F** sound.

Circle the things whose names begin with **J**.

Draw a line under the things whose names begin with **V**.

Draw a box around the things whose names begin **F**.

Skills: Auditory discrimination; Association of sounds and letters; Recognizing beginning sounds

Stacie needs help with her homework.
She has to match each letter to the picture that begins with that sound.
Stacie is thinking about the **P** sound, the **G** sound, the **Y** sound, and the **Z** sound.
Help Stacie by drawing lines from each letter to the correct picture.

P G   Y Z

Skills: Auditory discrimination; Association of sounds and letters; Recognizing beginning sounds

Barbie is sending thank you notes to her friends!
She must get the right note in each envelope.
Each note has a **lowercase** letter.
Each envelope has an **uppercase** letter.
Draw lines to connect the notes and envelopes with matching letters.

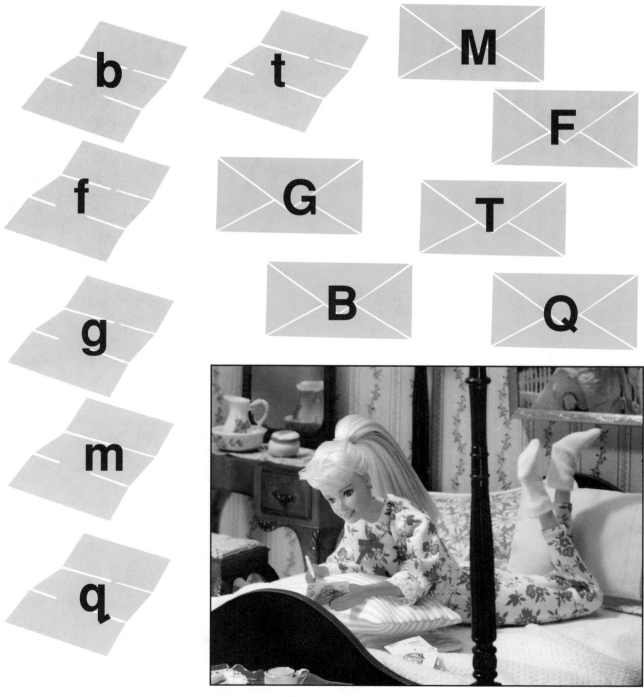

Skills: Letter recognition; Matching uppercase and lowercase letters; Friendship; Consideration

Words and More Words

Children look, listen, and learn new words every day! In this chapter, Barbie and her friends encourage them to practice skills sure to make their vocabularies grow. These include:

- understanding word concepts
- matching pictures to simple words
- seeing correspondences between spoken and written words
- practicing left-to-right reading
- understanding pairs of related words
- identifying opposites.

Vocabulary

large

small

Opposites

in

out

Left and Right

left

right

Kira is exploring the zoo with some friends.
Kira is big. Her friends are small.
Some animals are big and others are small.
Look at the pairs of animals.
Circle the animals that are **big.**
Draw a line under the animals that are **small**.

BIG SMALL

Skills: Vocabulary development; Making comparisons; Recognizing big and small; Nature; Curiosity

Ken helps in the furniture store.
He is arranging things by size.
Help him by drawing an **X** on the **big** things.
Draw a line under the **medium** things.
Draw a circle around the **small** things.

BIG
MEDIUM
SMALL

Skills: Vocabulary development; Making comparisons; Recognizing big, medium, and small; Responsibility

© 1999 Mattel, Inc.

Christie takes photographs of animals and their homes.
Some animals are in their homes and some are out.
Look at each animal and its home.
Circle the animals that are **in** their homes.
Draw a line under animals that are **out** of their homes.

IN   OUT

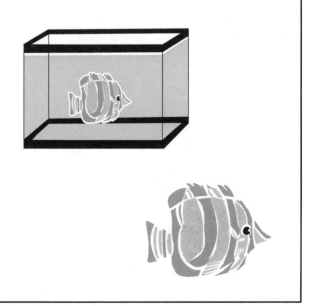

Skills: Vocabulary development; Recognizing in and out; Nature

Barbie is teaching gymnastics.
Some of her friends are up high on
the equipment and some are down low.
Look at each girl doing gymnastics.
Circle the girls that are **up** on the equipment and
draw a line under the girls that are **down**.

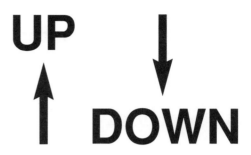

Skills: Vocabulary development; Recognizing up and down; Fitness

Ken is playing on his soccer team.
He is kicking the ball to your right.
Look at the things below.
Circle everything that is facing **right.**

RIGHT →

Skills: Vocabulary development; Recognizing directionality; Fitness

Cowgirl Barbie is herding the ranch animals into the corral.
She is pointing to your left.
Look at the ranch animals below.
Circle all the animals that are walking to the **left.**

LEFT

Skills: Vocabulary development; Recognizing directionality; Responsibility

Barbie and her friends are having a party.
Some girls wear short dresses,
and some wear long dresses.
Some boys have brown hair,
and some boys have blonde hair.
Draw a picture of a party you might have.
Tell what is the **same** in the picture.
Tell what is **different** in the picture.

Skills: Observing differences; Using new vocabulary; Creativity; Friendship

ANSWER KEY

Page 8

Barbie and Teresa are good friends.
They are going shopping together to buy matching outfits.
Look at the clothes on this page.
Draw lines to show which clothes are exactly the **same.**

Page 11

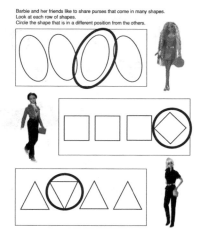

Barbie and her friends like to share purses that come in many shapes.
Look at each row of shapes.
Circle the shape that is in a different position from the others.

Page 9

Kelly is collecting shells on the beach.
Look at each group of shells she found.
Cross out the one that is **different** in each group.

Page 12

Barbie is a beautiful ballerina!
She needs strong muscles for dancing.
Look at all her costumes.
Draw lines to match each picture with the correct shadow.

Page 10

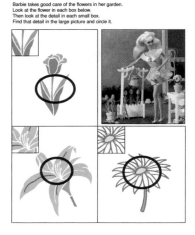

Barbie takes good care of the flowers in her garden.
Look at the flower in each box below.
Then look at the detail in each small box.
Find that detail in the large picture and circle it.

Page 13

Barbie is Ken's track coach.
She is helping him get ready to run in a race.
Look at what she brought along.
Circle one object in each box that is **different** from the others.

ANSWER KEY

Page 16

Ken is helping his neighbor to clean out the garage.
Look at each group of objects he found.
Circle the two pictures that go together.

Page 17

Stacie is packing her bookbag for school.
She doesn't want to forget anything important!
Circle the pictures of things she should take to school.
Draw an **X** over the things she should leave at home.

Page 18

Barbie, Ken, and Stacie are having lunch at their campsite.
Stacie is roasting marshmallows for everyone.
Circle all the other things they might eat on a camping trip.

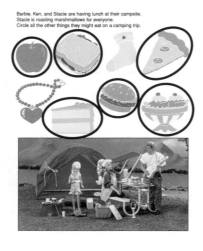

Page 19

Kelly is smaller than Barbie.
Kelly wants to know which pets are smaller.
Look at each pair of animals.
Circle the one that is **smaller**.
Draw a line under the one that is **larger**.

Page 20

Teresa works in a hair salon. She counts the supplies every day.
Look at each group of pictures.
Draw a line under the group in each box that shows **more**.
Circle the group that shows **less**.

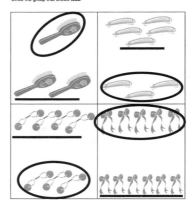

Page 21

It's moving day! Ken is helping Barbie by loading up the car.
Look at each picture.
Circle the pictures of things that could fit in the car.

ANSWER KEY

Page 34

Page 37

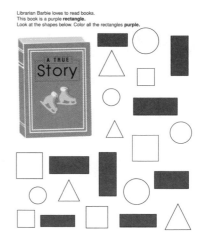

Page 35

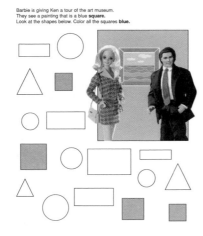

Page 38

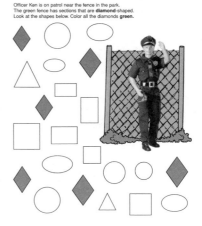

Page 36

Page 39

ANSWER KEY

Page 44

Barbie listens to the weather report on the radio.
What will the weather be?
Look at the weather pictures below.
Circle the number that tells how many of each you see.

Page 45

Barbie is buying a birthday gift for Stacie.
There are so many toys to choose from.
Count the toys on each shelf.
Write how many in the space at the end of the row.

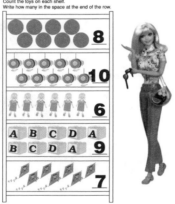

Page 46

Barbie follows safety rules when she rides her bike.
She watches out for people walking or driving cars.
She always wears her helmet. She obeys traffic signs.
Help her follow the correct path by tracing the
numbers in order from **1** to **10**.

Page 47

Christie is painting a picture for Barbie's house.
The numbers **1** to **10** are hidden in her studio.
Find and circle these numbers.

Page 50

Barbie is on her way to meet Ken.
Follow the dots from **A** to **Z** to find out
what Barbie's new car looks like.

Page 51

Barbie and Kira are helping to clean up the park.
They see things that begin with the **S** sound, the **T** sound, and the **B** sound.
Look at the picture below. Circle the things whose names begin with **S**.
Draw a line under the things whose names begin with **B**.
Draw a box around the things whose names begin with **T**.

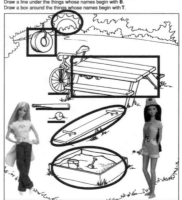

70

ANSWER KEY

Page 52

Barbie and Ken are camping.
They see things that begin with the **C** sound, the **R** sound, and the **W** sound.
Look at the picture below.
Circle the things whose names begin with **C**.
Draw a line under the things whose names begin with **W**.
Put a dot next to the things whose names begin with **R**.

Page 53

Kelly is drawing things that begin with the **K** sound,
the **H** sound, and the **M** sound.
Look at the pictures of things that she drew.
Write the sound you hear at the beginning of each pictured word.

Page 54

Barbie is exploring a trail.
She makes sure the nature trail is safe.
Look at the pictures of things Barbie saw on the trail.
They begin with the **D** sound, the **N** sound, and the **L** sound.
Write the sound you hear at the beginning of each pictured word.

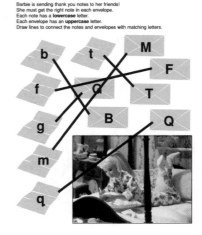

Page 55

Skipper is in the school yard. She notices things that begin with the **J** sound,
the **V** sound, and the **F** sound.
Circle the things whose names begin with **J**.
Draw a line under the things whose names begin with **V**.
Draw a box around the things whose names begin **F**.

Page 56

Stacie needs help with her homework.
She has to match each letter to the picture that begins with that sound.
Stacie is thinking about the **P** sound, the **G** sound, the **Y** sound, and the **Z** sound.
Help Stacie by drawing lines from each letter to the correct picture.

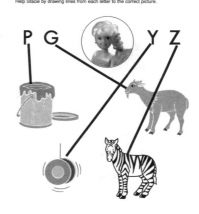

Page 57

Barbie is sending thank you notes to her friends!
She must get the right note in each envelope.
Each note has a **lowercase** letter.
Each envelope has an **uppercase** letter.
Draw lines to connect the notes and envelopes with matching letters.

ANSWER KEY

Page 60

Kira is exploring the zoo with some friends.
Kira is big. Her friends are small.
Some animals are big and others are small.
Look at the pairs of animals.
Circle the animals that are **big**.
Draw a line under the animals that are **small**.

BIG   SMALL

Page 61

Ken helps in the furniture store.
He is arranging things by size.
Help him by drawing an **X** on the **big** things.
Draw a line under the **medium** things.
Draw a circle around the **small** things.

**BIG
MEDIUM
SMALL**

Page 62

Christie takes photographs of animals and their homes.
Some animals are in their homes and some are out.
Look at each animal and its home.
Circle the animals that are **in** their homes.
Draw a line under animals that are **out** of their homes.

IN   OUT

Page 63

Barbie is teaching gymnastics.
Some of her friends are up high on
the equipment and some are down low.
Look at each girl doing gymnastics.
Circle the girls that are **up** on the equipment and
draw a line under the girls that are **down**.

**UP   ↓
↑   DOWN**

Page 64

Ken is playing on his soccer team.
He is kicking the ball to your right.
Look at the things below.
Circle everything that is facing **right**.

RIGHT →

Page 65

Cowgirl Barbie is herding the ranch animals into the corral.
She is pointing to your left.
Look at the ranch animals below.
Circle all the animals that are walking to the **left**.

LEFT
←

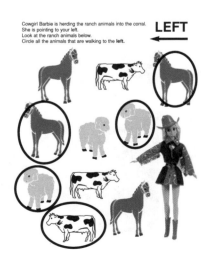

72